QUACKENSTEIN HATCHES A FAMILY

DANGER !
GRUMPY DUCK

¡ PELIGRO !
PATO MALHUMORADO

BY **SUDIPTA BARDHAN-QUALLEN**

ILLUSTRATED BY **BRIAN T. JONES**

Abrams Books for Young Readers

London

D1334989

The illustrations were made using acrylic paint on
illustration board and a bit of Photoshop here and there.

The Library of Congress has catalogued the hardcover edition of this book as follows:
Bardhan-Quallen, Sudipta.
Quackenstein hatches a family / Sudipta Bardhan-Quallen ; illustrated by Brian T. Jones.
p. cm.
Summary: A lonely duck at the zoo takes an egg home with him,
but when it hatches he is shocked by what emerges.
ISBN 978-0-8109-8973-3 (alk. paper)
[1. Stories in rhyme. 2. Ducks–Fiction. 3. Platypus–Fiction.
4. Animals–Infancy–Fiction. 5. Zoo animals–Fiction.
6. Humorous stories.] I. Jones, Brian T., ill. II. Title.
PZ8.3.B237Qu 2010
[E]–dc22
2009039757

Paperback ISBN 978-0-8109-9667-0

Book design by Chad W. Beckerman

Printed and bound in China
10 9 8 7 6 5 4 3 2 1

Abrams Books for Young Readers are available at special discounts when purchased in quantity for premiums
and promotions as well as fundraising or educational use. Special editions can also be created to specification.
For details, contact specialmarkets@abramsbooks.com or the address below.

THE ART OF BOOKS SINCE 1949
The Market Building
72-82 Rosebery Avenue
London, UK EC1R 4RW
www.abramsbooks.co.uk

To I, B, and S,
who have made
my heart sing. —S.B.

For Jenny, Fred, Jolynne,
Gus, and Lulu. —B.T.J.

In the darkest corner of the zoo
There stood a gloomy shack.

A nearby scrawl
Read:

KEEP OUT
ALL !!

JUST LEAVE ME
BE!
signed QUACK

Most creatures lived
In packs and herds,
In gaggles, bloats, and litters.

But all alone
There on his own
Poor Quackenstein grew bitter.

He was the hermit of the zoo
And faced a lonely struggle.
"It isn't fair!
My nest is bare!"
He had no one to snuggle.

Quack passed the nursery one day,
Where babies laughed and tumbled.

"Everyone has *some* someone,
Except for me," he mumbled.

He spied a small, secluded nook.
On impulse, he proceeded.
He bumped his head.
"A sign!" It read:

ORPHANED EGGS
HOMES NEEDED

Quack hatched a plan and crept ahead.
This duck would not be stopped.
On shaky legs,
He chose an egg

← NURSERY

RHINOCELOPE ⇨

And cackled:

I'LL
ADOPT!

Quack set it on his empty nest.
He kept his prize protected.
He'd gently coo,
"Dear ducky-poo,
You'll never be neglected!"

Then on one dark and stormy night,
The hour had arrived.
Quack heard a crack—

He stumbled back
And shouted:

Just then a small beak broke the shell!
Quack's heart thumped in his chest,
But then two paws
With sharp, curved claws
Thrust through and stabbed the nest.

"I've hatched . . . a monster! You're no duck,"
Quack screeched, and went quite pale.
The thing had fur
And legs with spurs
And some poor beaver's tail.

The creature lurched. Quack gasped,
"Stay back!"
The beast paid him no heed.
Quack tried to hide.
He ran outside,
Alarmed and rubber-kneed.

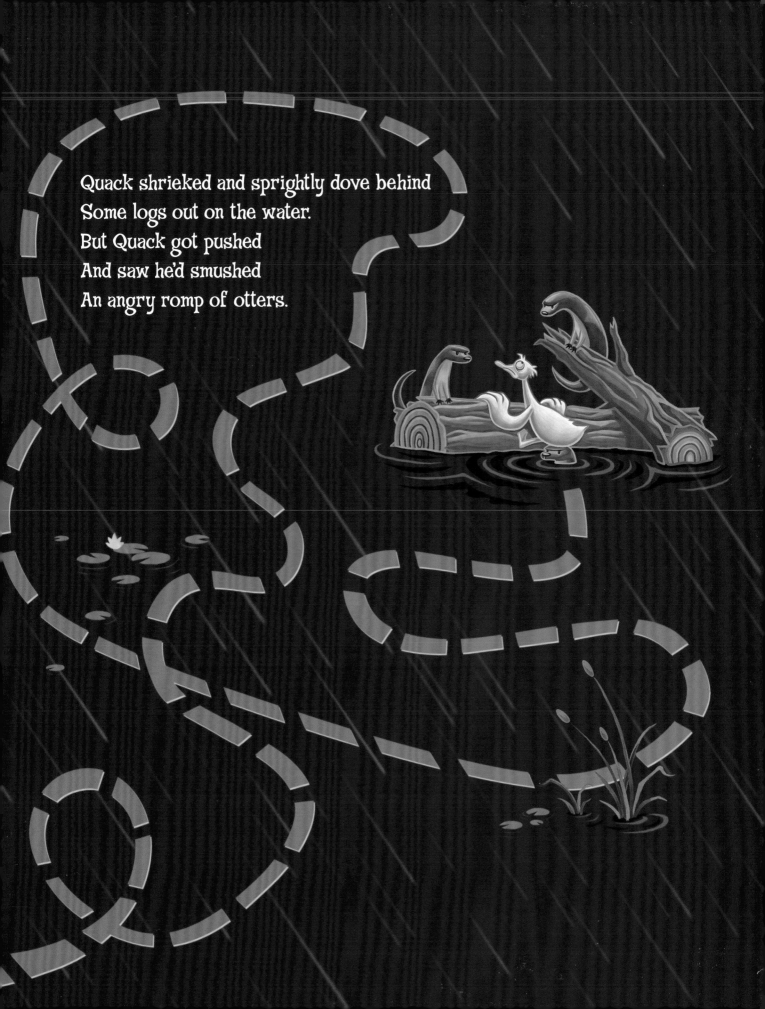

Quack shrieked and sprightly dove behind
Some logs out on the water.
But Quack got pushed
And saw he'd smushed
An angry romp of otters.

Drenched, the poor duck ducked behind
A mama heron reading.
Her babies screamed.
The thing's claws gleamed.
It leered and kept proceeding.

Quack shushed the rowdy heron hedge,
But birds just ran off blind.
They fled in shock
Toward cuddling crocs—
Soon all were intertwined.

Quack rashly rushed and promptly crushed
A hugging husk of hares.
"My fault!" Quack cried,
But then he spied
The monster's chilling glare.

So quickly Quack hid in a cave,
But there he'd made an error.
A furry shape
Blocked his escape.
"I'm trapped!" he screeched in terror.

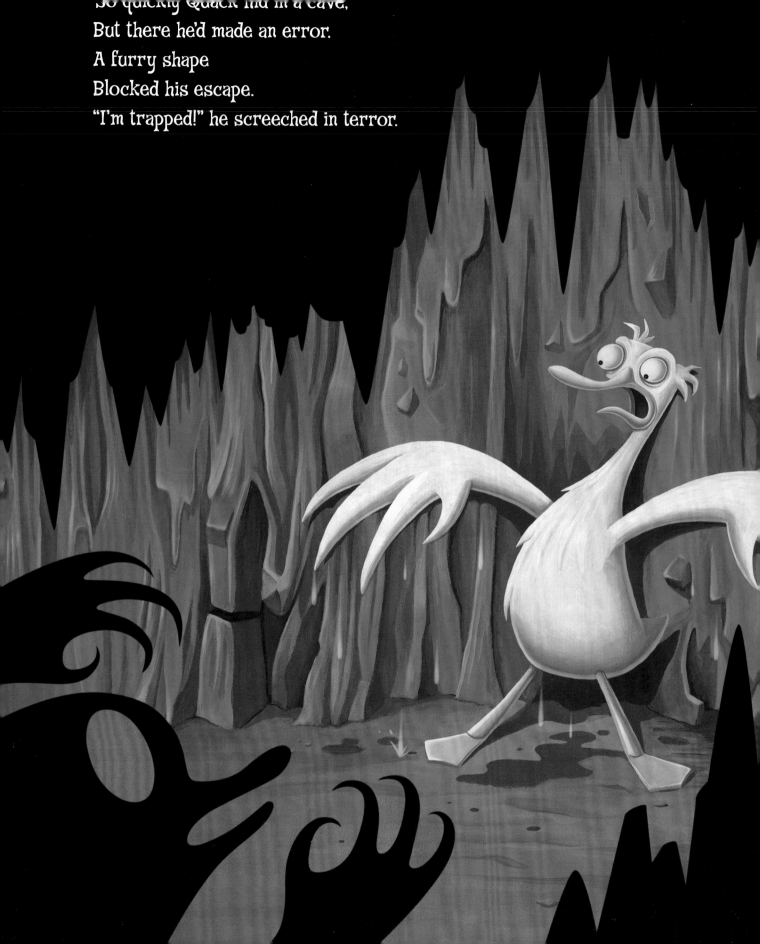

The thing then snarled, "Oh, there you are!"
It stalked the trembling fowl.
With sharp claws bared
And shoulders squared,
It leaped in with a growl!

Its paws soon squeezed the cringing duck,
And Quack thought, "This is BAD!"
His spirit broke
When someone spoke—

Quack could feel his cold heart melt,
And how his stomach fluttered.
"You chased me through
The great big zoo
To *be* with me?" he sputtered.

The creature beamed, "Yes, Daddy, yes!"
Quack's heart began to sing.
"Come, son," he squawked,
And off they walked,
In step, and paw in wing.

Then in the corner of the zoo
That once housed Quackenstein,
A space was cleared
And there appeared
A shiny brand-new sign.

WELCOME TO OUR HAPPY HOME

COME BY TO VISIT US.

LOVE, QUACK

it read.
Below, it said:

AND HIS SON,

PLATYPUS